P9-CQX-989

big

sit

Phonics Friends

Isabel's Favorite Things
The Sound of Short I

By Joanne Meier and Cecilia Minden

six

Published in the United States of America
by The Child's World®
PO Box 326
Chanhassen, MN 55317-0326
800-599-READ
www.childsworld.com

A special thank you to the Gaytan family for sharing your joy of traveling. Bon Voyage!

The Child's World®: Mary Berendes, Publishing Director

Editorial Directions, Inc.: E. Russell Primm, Editorial Director and Project Editor; Katie Marsico, Associate Editor; Judith Shiffer, Associate Editor and School Media Specialist; Linda S. Koutris, Photo Researcher and Selector

The Design Lab: Kathleen Petelinsek, Design and Page Production

Photographs ©: Photo setting and photography by Romie and Alice Flanagan/Flanagan Publishing Services: cover, 4, 8, 10, 12, 20; Corbis/Alese and Mort Pechter: 18; Corbis/Bo Zaunders: 16; Corbis/Danny Lehman: 6; Corbis/Scott Kerrigan: 14.

Library of Congress Cataloging-in-Publication Data
Meier, Joanne D.
Isabel's favorite things : the sound of short I / by Joanne Meier and Cecilia Minden.
p. cm. — (Phonics friends)
Summary: In simple text featuring the short "I" sound, Isabel and her mother discuss an upcoming family trip on a ship.
ISBN 1-59296-314-5 (library bound : alk. paper) [1. English language—Phonetics. 2. Reading.] I. Minden, Cecilia. II. Title. III. Series.
PZ7.M5148Is 2004
[E]—dc22 2004002197

Note to parents and educators:

The Child's World® has created Phonics Friends with the goal of exposing children to engaging stories and pictures that assist in phonics development. The books in the series will help children learn the relationships between the letters of written language and the individual sounds of spoken language. This contact helps children learn to use these relationships to read and write words.

The books in this series follow a similar format. An introductory page, to be read by an adult, introduces the child to the phonics feature, or sound, that will be highlighted in the book. Read this page to the child, stressing the phonic feature. Help the student learn how to form the sound with her mouth. The Phonics Friends story and engaging photographs follow the introduction. At the end of the story, word lists categorize the feature words into their phonic element. Additional information on using these lists is on The Child's World® Web site listed at the top of this page.

Each book in this series has been carefully written to meet specific readability requirements. Close attention has been paid to elements such as word count, sentence length, and vocabulary. Readability formulas measure the ease with which the text can be read and understood. Each Phonics Friends book has been analyzed using the Spache readability formula. For more information on this formula, as well as the levels for each of the books in this series please visit The Child's World® Web site.

Reading research suggests that systematic phonics instruction can greatly improve students' word recognition, spelling, and comprehension skills. The Phonics Friends series assists in the teaching of phonics by providing students with important opportunities to apply their knowledge of phonics as they read words, sentences, and text.

The letter *i* makes two sounds.

The long sound of *i* sounds like *i* as in:

bike and *ripe*.

The short sound of *i* sounds like *i* as in:

itch and *dig*.

In this book you will read words that have the short *i* sound as in:

six, fish, pig, and *trip*.

LATITUDES
THE FREEDOM OF CRUISING:
INTRODUCING "PRIDE OF AMERICA"
America

Isabel is six years old.

Her family is planning a trip.

They are going on a big ship.

embark

"What can we bring on the ship?"

asks Isabel.

"Can we bring our kitten?"

asks Isabel.

"No, the kitten might get sick,"

says Mother.

"Can I bring my toy pig?"

asks Isabel.

"No, it is too big to fit,"

says Mother.

"What can we do on the ship?"

asks Isabel.

"We can watch the big fish swim,"

says Mother.

"We can skip on the deck.

Be careful not to trip!"

says Mother.

"We can sit on the deck.
The sun will feel good!"
says Mother.

"We will have a great trip!"

says Isabel.

Fun Facts

Most pigs are big, but the largest was an animal named Big Bill, who weighed in at 2,552 pounds (1,158 kilograms)! Scientists consider pigs to be fairly intelligent animals and believe they are even better at learning tricks than most dogs. Many pigs live on farms, but people often keep potbellied pigs as pets. Perhaps you've heard of guinea pigs. These furry pets aren't pigs at all–they're rodents! People believe they may originally have been called pigs because they make noises similar to the squeal of a pig.

Maybe you've taken a trip on an airplane or even on a cruise ship. How would you like to go for a trip on a hot air balloon? In 1999, Bertrand Piccard and Brian Jones traveled around the world in a hot air balloon. The trip took them 20 days.

Activity

Planning a Trip with Your Family

It's fun to visit places far away from home, but you don't always have to get on a plane or drive far in the car to plan a fun trip! Talk to your parents about organizing a trip to the zoo or a nearby museum. If you live near a wilderness area, consider planning a hiking trip through the woods.

To Learn More

Books

About the Sound of Short I

Klingel, Cynthia, and Robert B. Noyed. *Little Bit: The Sound of Short I.* Chanhassen, Minn.: The Child's World, 2000.

About Fish

Goldfinger, Jennifer P. *A Fish Named Spot.* Boston: Little, Brown, 2001.

Pfister, Marcus, and J. Alison James (translator). *Rainbow Fish 1, 2, 3.* New York: North-South Books, 2002.

About Pigs

McPhail, David M. *Pigs Aplenty, Pigs Galore!* New York: Dutton Children's Books, 1993.

Walton, Rick, and Jim Holder (illustrator). *Pig, Pigger, Piggest.* Salt Lake City: Gibbs-Smith, 1997.

About Trips

McMullan, Kate, and Mavis Smith (illustrator). *Fluffy's Funny Field Trip.* New York: Scholastic, 2001.

Owain, Bell (illustrator). *Thomas and the School Trip.* New York: Random House, 2003.

Web Sites

Visit our home page for lots of links about the Sound of Short I:

http://www.childsworld.com/links.html

Note to Parents, Teachers, and Librarians: We routinely check our Web links to make sure they're safe, active sites—so encourage your readers to check them out!

Short I Feature Words

Proper Names

Isabel

Feature Words in Initial Position

is	it

Feature Words in Medial Position

big	sick
fit	sit
kitten	six
pig	

Feature Words with Blends and Digraphs

fish	swim
ship	trip
skip	

About the Authors

Joanne Meier, PhD, has worked as an elementary school teacher and university professor. She earned her BA in early childhood education from the University of South Carolina, and her MEd and PhD in education from the University of Virginia. She currently works as a literacy consultant for schools and private organizations. Joanne Meier lives with her husband Eric, and spends most of her time chasing her two daughters, Kella and Erin, and her two cats, Sam and Gilly, in Charlottesville, Virginia.

Cecilia Minden, PhD, directs the Language and Literacy Program at the Harvard Graduate School of Education. She is a reading specialist with classroom and administrative experience in grades K–12. She earned her PhD in reading education from the University of Virginia. Cecilia and her husband Dave Cupp enjoy sharing their love of reading with their granddaughter Chelsea.